A True Champion

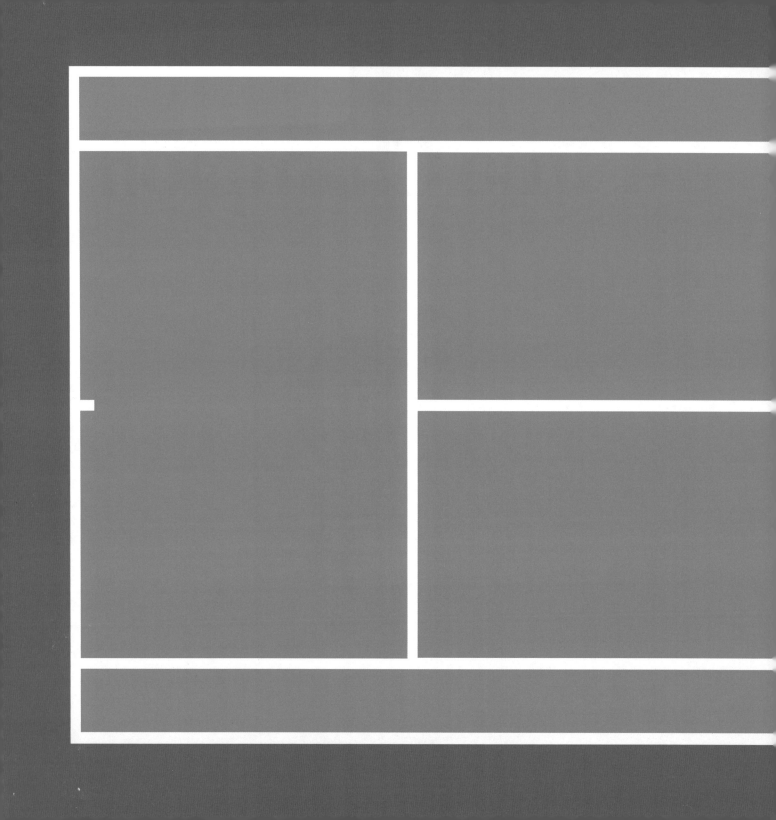

First published in February 2021 by Famous Books
Email: hello@acetennisbooks.com
www.acetennisbooks.com

ISBN: 978-0-9560255-31

Text and illustrations copyright Puneet Bhandal 2021
Moral rights asserted.

A CIP catalogue record for this book is available from the British Library.

A True Champion

By Puneet Bhandal   Illustrated by Saad Ali

FAMOUS BOOKS

There Can Only Be One Winner

Storm had butterflies in his tummy.

It was the last day of term at the Spaceship Tennis Academy and he was competing for the Rocket Trophy. The Academy's motto was loud and clear – *There Can Only Be One Winner*. It made Storm feel more nervous.

"Don't think about winning or losing," said his mum. "Try your best and enjoy the match."

The stadium had filled up with people, all eager to see the finalists play. The Umpire took his seat. "Ladies and gentlemen," he announced. "Please welcome Storm from Great Britain and Logan from the USA."

Storm and his opponent made their way to the net. The Tournament Director explained the rules. "The first player to get ten points wins the game. It's best of three, so you need two games to win the match."

"Good luck, Logan," said Storm. "Thanks, you too," he replied.

As Storm made his way to the baseline, he could hear Logan's mum and brother chanting Logan's name.

"Block it out," Storm told himself. "Focus on the match."

He stopped for a moment to look around the stadium. He had never played in front of such a big crowd before. There was so much noise – people were whistling, clapping and cheering loudly.

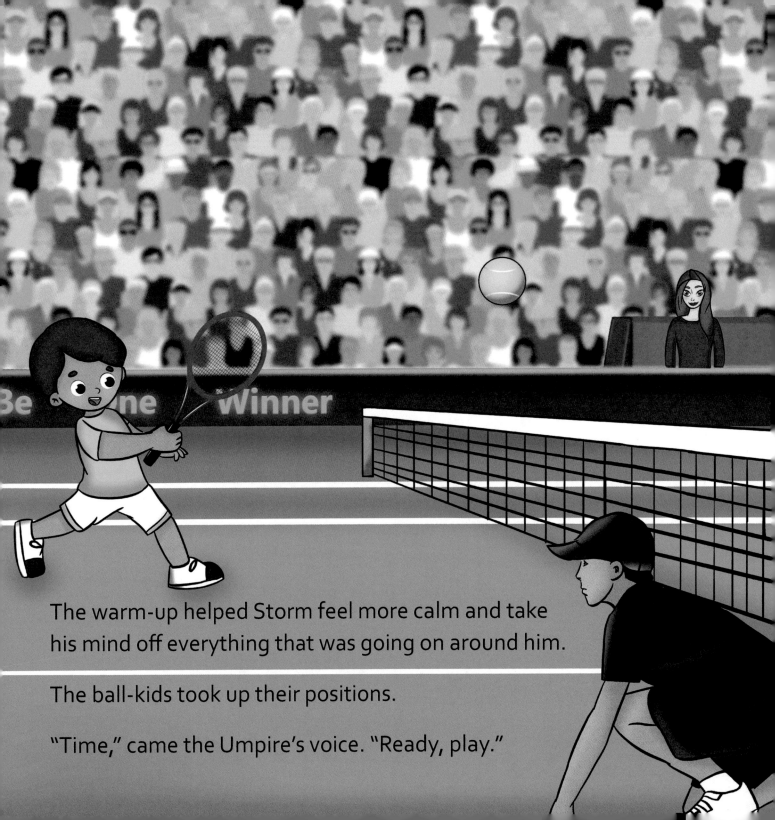

The warm-up helped Storm feel more calm and take his mind off everything that was going on around him.

The ball-kids took up their positions.

"Time," came the Umpire's voice. "Ready, play."

Storm bounced the ball on the baseline as he prepared to serve. He then tossed it in the air and hit it as hard as he could. The ball hit the net.

He took a deep breath. Storm served again but this time, the ball landed out. It was a double fault.

He lost the point.

Thankfully, the next serve landed in...

... but Logan outplayed Storm with amazing shots.

Logan was the first to win ten points...

STORM GB	07	00
	POINTS	GAMES
LOGAN USA	10	01

... which meant he won the first game.

The boys walked over to their benches for a break. Storm looked over at the wall stating *There Can Only Be One Winner*. It was glaring at him.

He then noticed the shiny, gold Rocket Trophy. He wanted to win it so badly that he felt terrified of losing. "Time," announced the Umpire.

Storm decided to change his mindset – he vowed to give it his all. He wasn't going to lose this match without playing his best tennis.

He hit some superb shots, including a volley that Logan had no answer for. The audience applauded Storm's brave play when he won the second game. "Yes, you can do it!" he shouted with confidence.

It was time for the third and
final game – the one that
would decide the winner.

"Relax," Storm told himself.
"One point at a time."

Storm returned
Logan's powerful
serve with a
wondrous backhand.

Both players seemed
fearless as they hit
the ball back and
forth in some long
and tiring rallies.

Then, unexpectedly, Logan hit the most sublime drop shot. Storm was on the service line, totally unprepared for it.

The scoreboard flashed: *Championship Point*.

Logan's supporters screamed in excitement. He needed just one more point to win the match and the Rocket Trophy.

"Overruled," said the Umpire.
"The ball was *in*."

Storm walked over to the
Umpire's chair. "My ball was out."

"Are you sure?" asked the Umpire.

"Yes, I saw clearly. My ball was out," repeated Storm. "The line judge was correct."

"Well, in that case," smiled the Umpire, "game and match – Logan!"

Logan's family and fans jumped up and down with joy. He stood with arms aloft in the centre of the court, enjoying his biggest victory.

Storm's mum ran down and gave her son a big hug.

"Sorry I lost, mum," he said.

"I'm so proud of you," she smiled.

At the presentation ceremony, Logan held up his trophy while Storm showed off his runner-up plate.

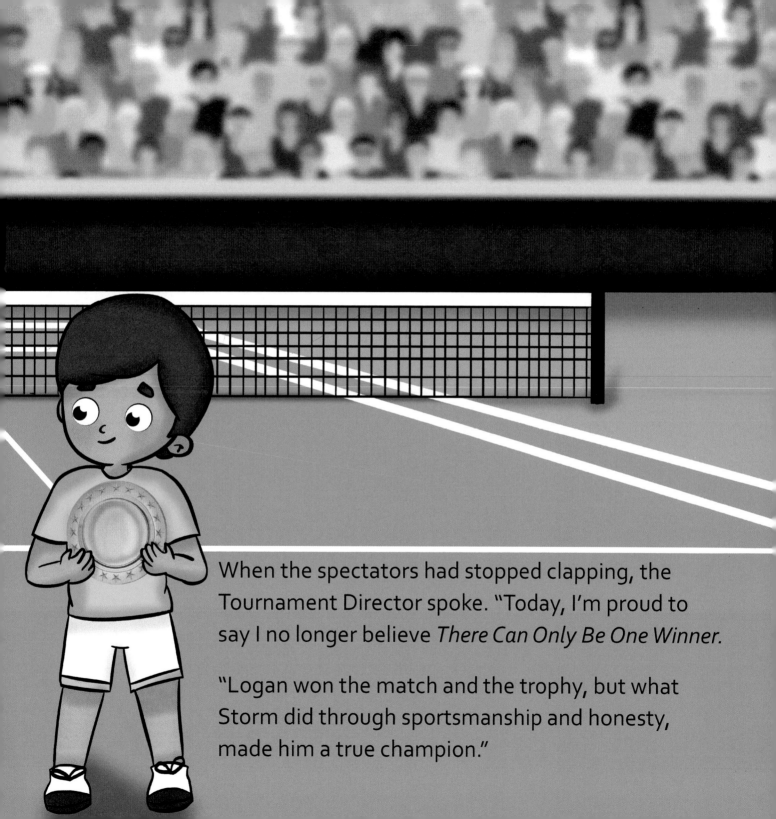

When the spectators had stopped clapping, the Tournament Director spoke. "Today, I'm proud to say I no longer believe *There Can Only Be One Winner.*

"Logan won the match and the trophy, but what Storm did through sportsmanship and honesty, made him a true champion."

Glossary

Backhand A stroke that is hit with the back of the racket face, and back of the hand.

Ball-kid A boy or girl who retrieves balls and supplies players with them.

Baseline Line at farthest ends of the court, marking the boundary of the playing area.

Drop shot Where the ball is hit relatively softly, and lands just over and close to the net.

Double fault Two serving faults in a row, causing the player serving to lose the point.

Forehand A shot made by swinging the racket across the body, the hand moving palm-first.

Line judge Person responsible for calling the lines on the tennis court. There can be several line judges in a match.

Rally A sequence of back and forth shots between players, within a point. Plural of rally is rallies.

Return The immediate stroke made by the receiver of a serve.

Serve The shot that begins each point, in which the server hits the ball after tossing it into the air.

Service line The line in the middle of the court that runs parallel to the net.

Tournament Director The official in charge of an event to ensure it runs smoothly.

Umpire The official in charge of announcing the score, enforcing the rules and making sure the match takes place in a spirit of fair play.

Volley A shot where the ball is struck before it bounces on the ground.